THROUGH WITH THE ZOO

Jacob Grant

FEIWEL AND FRIENDS
NEW YORK

A FEIWEL AND FRIENDS BOOK
An imprint of Macmillan Publishing Group, LLC

Our books may be purchased in bulk for promotional, educational, or business use.
Please contact your local bookseller or the Macmillan Corporate and Premium
Sales Department at (800) 221-7945 ext. 5442 or by e-mail
at MacmillanSpecialMarkets@macmillan.com.

Library of Congress Cataloging-in-Publication Data Available

ISBN: 978-1-250-10814-2

The art was drawn with charcoal and crayon and colored digitally.
Feiwel and Friends logo designed by Filomena Tuosto

First Edition: 2017

1 3 5 7 9 10 8 6 4 2

mackids.com

For Javi, our little goat.

Goat always dreamed of having space.
He didn't want hugs or rubs or anyone near him.

But Goat lived in a petting zoo.

Every day the small petting zoo was packed
with grabby little hands.

Goat looked out at the animals in the big zoo,

so safe from the wild children.

He would find a space out there just for him.

He tried living with a clingy koala.

He tried living with a nosy elephant.

Goat tried living with many animals,

but space was not an easy thing to find.

Finally Goat's search brought him to a lone tree. It was a quiet place that could be all his own.

Goat had more space than he'd ever dreamed of.

But was it too much?

He looked all around and knew that no one could get near him anymore.

No little faces, no little hands, no little hugs.

All that empty space was missing something.

Goat never thought he would miss the petting zoo.

But everyone needs a hug now and then.

Whenever Goat wanted a little space,
he knew just where to find it.